When they suffered,
he suffered also.
He sent his own
angel to save them.

ISAIAH 63:9

Rough Roads and Rainbows

Featuring G.T. and the Halo Express,
created by Doug and Debbie Kingsriter

Written by Ann Hibbard
Illustrated by Ann Neilsen

Published by Focus on the Family Publishing
Pomona, CA 91799

Distributed by Word Books, Dallas, Texas. Copyright © 1990 Focus on the Family Publishing
Scriptures quoted from *The Everyday Bible, New Century Version,* copyright © 1987,
1988 by Word Publishing, Dallas, Texas 75039. Used by permission.
G.T. and the Halo Express, Michael, Christy and Billy Baxter are copyrighted
by Doug and Debbie Kingsriter ©1987.

Library of Congress Catalog Card Number 90-081106
ISBN 0-929608-71-2
Cassette tapes featuring G.T. and the Halo Express in other adventures are also available by contacting
King Communications, P.O. Box 24472, Minneapolis, MN 55424 or your local Christian bookstore.

Sunlight streamed through a silvery crack in the big, gray clouds. A mist rose up from the wet street. The whole world smelled clean and new.

"Mmm, fresh air!" exclaimed Christy, taking a deep breath. "This must be what Noah felt like when he finally got out of the ark. I thought it would never stop raining."

"Yeah, let's hit the road!" Her brother Michael grabbed his bike and popped the kickstand. "Harrison Street Park, here we come!"

Christy tucked a brown lunch sack in her bike basket and hopped on her bike.

"Looks like it'll be smooth sailing," predicted Christy, pedaling down the glistening street. Her pigtails floated behind her like crepe paper streamers.

"Just a few puddles. No problem," Michael agreed.

The road dropped off ahead of them, down a long, steep hill and disappeared around a curve.

"Get ready for Danger Hill," Christy said, gulping.

"I've ridden it hundreds of times," Michael exaggerated. "Let's go!" He shot off down the hill.

"Be careful turning onto Stone Road. It's pretty bumpy," Christy called after him.

The wind whipped her clothes and stung her cheeks as she flew down Danger Hill. She rounded the curve just in time to see Michael swerve onto Stone Road, going full speed.

Suddenly Michael's bike flipped, throwing him over the handlebars. Catapulting through the air, he landed in a heap on the road.

Christy sped to the scene of the accident and rushed over to him.

"Are you all right?" she gasped.

Michael looked up and slowly started to rise. To their amazement, someone was underneath him. There, lying flat on the road, was the dusty figure of their guardian angel, Good Tidings.

"G.T., what are you doing there?!" they cried in unison, helping him to his feet.

Chuckling, G.T. brushed off his robe and readjusted his halo. "I'm trying to keep Michael from hurting himself!"

"That was a close one," Michael admitted with a sigh of relief. Then he thoughtfully added: "I guess I was going a little too fast."

"Michael, look at your bike!" Christy cried out.

The handlebars were twisted, and the front tire looked like a deflated basketball.

"Oh, great! Now what are we going to do?" Michael exclaimed.

"Never fear, G.T.'s here!" their angelic friend declared. He rolled up his sleeves and marched over to the bike.

Taking the twisted handlebars in his hands, he bent them back into shape as easily as if they were putty.

"Wow! How did you do that?" Michael marveled.

G.T. grinned. "Angels have a special kind of strength. Now watch this!"

He knelt down and put his mouth over the tire valve. Puffing out his cheeks, he blew. The tire filled with air right before their eyes.

"Here you go!" G.T. said, sounding just like the man at the gas station.

"Thanks, G.T.," said Michael. "You're the greatest! And thanks for saving me. I'll be more careful."

Christy gave G.T. a big hug.

"I guess I should let you get going, but I feel like I'm forgetting something," G.T. puzzled, scratching his head. "Oh, yes—the message. How could I have forgotten!"

"Message? What message?" they questioned.

"Now where did I put it?" G.T. muttered to himself, feeling in all his pockets. "Wait, here it is. I tucked it behind my beeper."

G.T. unfolded a thin, crisp paper of the palest blue. Michael and Christy rubbed their eyes and stared. Something was moving on the paper. It looked like fluffy white clouds, swirling and churning. Sparkles of color shot out from the clouds like diamonds in the snow.

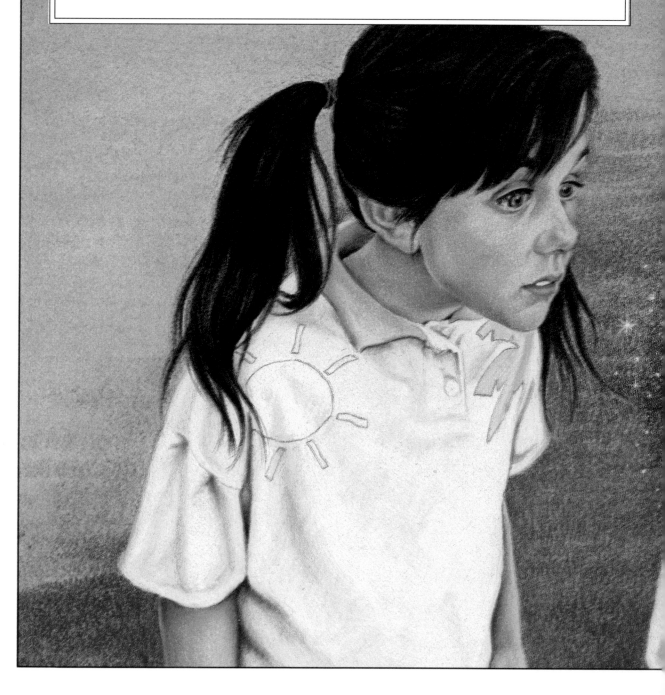

"Ahem," G.T. cleared his thoat, then read:
"Dear Christy and Michael,
When the road is rough, don't be worried or afraid. I will
be with you and will give you the strength that you need.
Never forget that I love you.
Your friend,
Jesus"

"Wow!" Michael and Christy breathed.

With eyes round as saucers, they watched in amazement as the paper began to fade. Soon all that was left were the sparkles of light. One by one the sparkles also vanished.

"It's gone," whispered Michael.

"Not gone," said G.T. "It's inside of you. Jesus gave you a wonderful promise, and it will never disappear."

"I'll never forget this," Christy said solemnly.

"Well, just in case, look for the rainbow. That's God's reminder that he always keeps his promises," G.T. explained, pointing upward.

High in the sky, they saw a faint band of color. When they looked down again, G.T. had vanished.

"I feel like I can tackle anything now!" exclaimed Christy, mounting her bike.

Michael let out a whoop and charged ahead, this time riding more carefully on the bumpy surface of Stone Road. Their bikes rattled and clanked as they pedaled up a small hill.

At the top of the hill, they paused to catch their breath.

"Boy, I'm working up an appetite!" announced Michael, casting a longing glance at the sack in Christy's basket.

"We've still got a ways to go," Christy pointed out.

"I'm ready," Michael declared.

They hurled themselves down the hill, ducking their heads to avoid the branches that hung low over the road.

"Whoaaa!" they cried as they rounded the bend.

Just a few feet ahead, the road disappeared into murky brown water.

"All that rain must have made the pond overflow," remarked Christy gloomily.

"Now how are we going to make it up the big hill?" wailed Michael, staring at where the road reappeared on the other side of the overflow.

"First we've got to get around this water, Michael," Christy reminded him.

"We could walk our bikes through it," Michael suggested brightly.

"Uh-uh!" Christy replied, shaking her head. "It could be deep. Besides, no telling what slimy creatures live in that disgusting water."

They both turned to the bank on the other side of the road. It was thick with thorny branches.

"It's impossible," Michael said hopelessly.

"Maybe not," said Christy. She parked her bike and began to walk along the thicket.

"Hey, Michael, come here. There's a path!" exclaimed Christy, pointing into the tangle of bushes.

"You call that a path?" remarked Michael.

"Well, it looks like somebody has gone through here ahead of us. Let's try it!"

Christy retrieved her bike, pushing it up the bank and into the thicket. Michael followed, looking doubtful.

Slowly they picked their way through the heavy underbrush. Branches snapped around them like rubber bands. But the faint path led them around the patch of thorny bushes.

"Look, Christy, we're on the other side of the water!" cried Michael.

"Now for the big hill," declared Christy. "We'll just have to walk our bikes up it, I guess."

"It feels like we're going straight up," Michael puffed when they were about halfway up the hill.

Then they heard a low bark. A huge, black dog darted down a driveway, right toward them. His mouth hung open, showing two rows of sharp teeth.

"Oh, no. It's Fang!" moaned Michael.

"F-F-Fang?" stuttered Christy, walking her bike faster.

"He's mean. Really mean," Michael gulped. "And he hates bikers."

They broke into a run. Fang reached the end of the driveway and stopped abruptly, almost as if he were on a leash.

"Look, Christy! Fang stopped!" Michael sputtered, trying to catch his breath.

"Thank goodness!" Christy wheezed. She breathed hard, holding her side. "Michael, I don't think I can make it."

"Sure you can, Christy. It's downhill all the way from here," Michael encouraged her. "See?"

Sure enough, they had made it to the top of the hill. At the bottom and down another street, the playground glimmered in the sunlight.

The sight of their goal gave them a new burst of energy. Down the hill they raced like bolts of lightning. Faster and faster they sped.

Splash! Christy hit a big puddle. Water sprayed everywhere, and her bike slid out from underneath her. She landed with a giant plop in the middle of the water.

Michael ran to her rescue.

"Are you hurt?" he asked, helping her up.

"I-I don't think so," Christy answered bravely. She surveyed her muddy clothes. "Boy, am I a mess!"

"I'll get a napkin from the lunch bag," suggested Michael. "Oh, no, our lunch!"

They watched as the bag slowly sank to the bottom of the puddle.

Michael snatched it out. But brown water streamed from the sack. He carefully set it in Christy's bike basket and wheeled the bike over to Christy.

"We sure have had rough roads today," Michael observed as they rode into the park.

They looked around with dismay. No kids were in sight, but water was everywhere! The equipment was soaked, and the ground underneath was covered with puddles as big as lakes.

"I don't believe it!" Michael said gloomily. "What else can go wrong?"

"Maybe things will dry out as we eat our lunch," Christy suggested, trying to sound cheerful. They sat down on a bench and dug into their lunch bag. The sandwiches they pulled out were like sponges sopped with muddy water.

"Oh, yuck! So much for the sandwiches," Michael said. "Let's hope the cookies are dry—I'm starving!"

But all that was left of the cookies were soggy brown crumbs.

"What a disaster!" Christy sighed. They gave each other a glum look.

"Where is G.T. when we need him?" muttered Michael.

"Wait a minute," Christy blurted out. "That message—Jesus promised he'd give us the strength that we needed…and so far, it's worked."

"But what can he do about a ruined lunch?" Michael returned hopelessly.

"What was it that G.T. said?" Christy pondered. "Oh, yeah. Look for the rainbow. Michael, look!"

The biggest, brightest rainbow they had ever seen was in front of them. And it reached all the way to the ground!

They ran as fast as they could over to the rainbow. The colors shimmered and danced. Instinctively, they reached out their hands. Purple, blue, green, yellow, orange and red—their hands turned various colors as the children moved them across the rainbow.

"Michael, let's step inside the rainbow," Christy whispered, her eyes shining.

Michael nodded. First one foot, then the other.

Immediately they were surrounded by a shower of colorful sparkles. The children laughed and jumped and danced. They slid from one band of color to the next. They had to try everything. They twirled each other around, and the colors spun like a kaleidoscope.

Laughing and panting, they paused to catch their breath.

"Listen, Christy, I hear a band. There's a big crowd over there!"

"The rainbow led us here where we could see them. Look, they're all blue!" Christy squealed with delight.

"No, they're all red!" laughed Michael.

"Everything looks so different in the rainbow," Christy breathed.

Then she squinted. "Look, Michael, a hot dog vendor is over there."

"I wish I'd brought my allowance," Michael said, thrusting his hands in his pockets. "Hey, I've got a quarter in my pocket!"

"Me, too!" exclaimed Christy, bringing out a shiny coin. It glinted all the colors of the rainbow.

Christy and Michael ran like the wind.

The sign read, "HOT DOGS 50 CENTS."

"I guess we'll just have to split one, Michael," Christy said.

"One hot dog, please," she said to the hot dog vendor.

"Sure thing," he mumbled. He reached down and put up a sign that had fallen on the ground. It said, "TWO FOR THE PRICE OF ONE."

"Make that two hot dogs…please!" Michael piped up. "And hold the relish!"

"Great band, huh?" Christy commented, happily munching her hot dog.

"Yeah," agreed Michael between bites. "If I didn't know better, I'd say they look an awful lot like G.T.'s band, the Halo Express!"

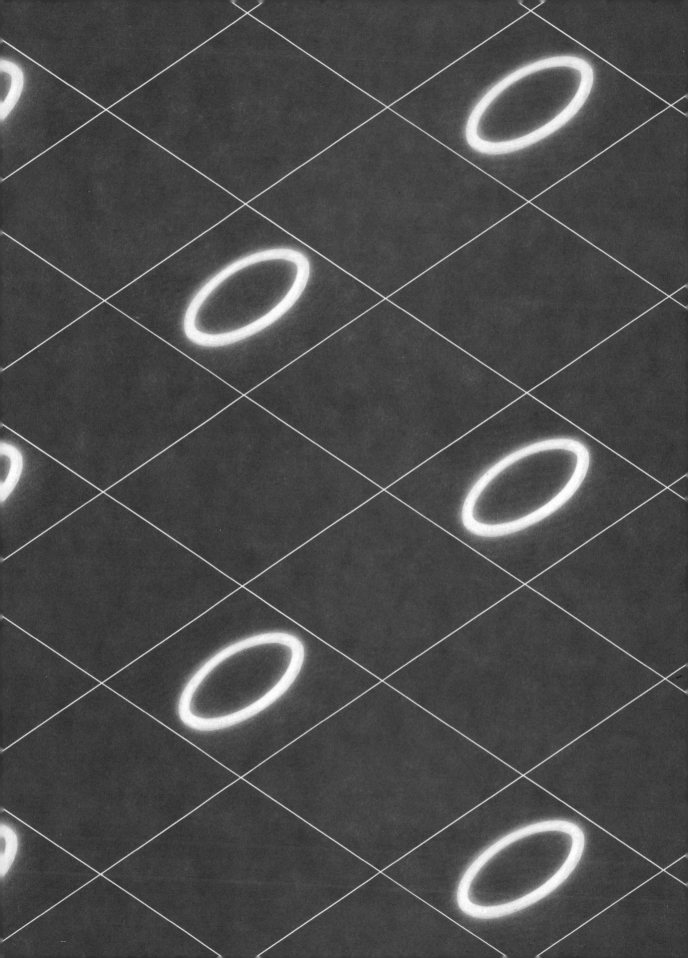